ZOMBIE ZERO
THE SHORT STORIES

THE ZOMBIE KILLERS

Zombie Zero: The Short Stories
The Zombie Killers

ISBN-13: 978-1-944916-83-1
ISBN-10: 1-944916-83-0

www.SuddenInsightPublishing.com
Indie publishing for the Indie Author

ZOMBIE ZERO
THE SHORT STORIES

THE ZOMBIE KILLERS

J.K. NORRY

FOREWORD

It could be argued that I am enjoying 'The Year of the Zombie' a bit too much; there's no indication that I'm not enjoying it enough. As a huge fan of fireworks, my best metaphor would be a finale that lasts forever. Or a year, anyhow. Never mind, there's no need for metaphor; I simply love zombies!

Of course, I don't want to have them over for dinner or anything...but I do love what they have to say, and I understand what they are here to do...so we're cool. As long as they don't try to eat me or anything.

So what do the zombies have to say that made me so eager to tell their stories this year? Well, there is a deeper meaning to all of this. There is also deeper meaning to each of these individuals that the stories are about. In fact, there's so much deeper meaning flying around that I had to start my own 'member's only' club. It's a secret society, but anyone who follows the breadcrumbs from my books can find their way to it; also, we do advertise it a little. See how I have trouble taking even secrecy seriously?

Check out these stories, if they are the first you have read, without any concern for whether or not you're reading them out of order. There won't be any spoilers in these stories or the commentary between them if you want to go back and read the others later. If you want to read everything in the 'Zombie Zero' world in the sequence I would have you read it, you'll have to go back a bit. This being the fourth volume in the short stories collection, you will want to read the other three first. Before that, you'll want to read 'Zombie Zero: The First Zombie'. Once you're done with all that, it can really be up to you if you finish the short stories or the long ones first.

'Zombie Zero: The Last Zombie' released right before this book, if you want to read the conclusion to all this. If you'd rather hang out with the apocalypse for a while longer before it finally ends, there are two more short story volumes in this collection. They occur during the events of the first book, although two release after the last book.

If you're just here for great zombie stories, hop to the pages with titles at the top of them. For those of you that like it when I have more to say before we get started...

I have more to say before we get started.

ABOUT THE SHORT STORIES

At first I thought these short stories would be a nice complementary collection to the longer books. Later, I realized that they were playing a much more important role in making the world of 'Zombie Zero' come to life for both me and my readers. I realized that a head without a body is just as incomplete as a body without a head, and made my peace with how much these stories were coming to mean to me.

As much as I like to poke fun at myself, and plant my tongue firmly in cheek when I write sometimes, I take my job as an author very seriously. This project turned out to be the perfect outpicturing of all of those parts of me, and the short stories really crystallized some of them. I wanted to make sure that these stories were fun, and entertaining, and even gruesome at times...but they had to have something more to offer as well, for the folks that have come to expect that of me.

That meant finding the kind of characters that I'm drawn to within this world that was so meaningfully falling apart.

It wasn't hard; many people are motivated by their own deeper meaning, and the apocalypse only heightens that motivation. There was a call to dig deeper into myself, to plant my consciousness more firmly in this world, and to look for the stories within the story that would best serve both my readers and me. It's the kind of work I delight in, and mostly it requires a lot of time spent staring at the company Appletop and making an endless series of tiny subtle movements.

The characters in these stories were some of the first to step forward, and capture my attention. There had been a brief glimpse of them in 'Zombie Zero: The First Zombie', and I had been intrigued by the implied back story. When I asked for more, I knew right away that these would be some of the short stories. This special group of people had some meaningful things to say, and I wanted to hear them. Also, they're pretty super badass; I wanted to see that too.

Of course, making more than two books meant making more than two covers. The artist we had commissioned to do the main two book covers was happy to help, and we were excited to see what he came up with. As he was part of all of this coming together, I'd like to tell you about Sean Harrington.

ODE TO SEAN HARRINGTON

There was never any concern on our end that we would not be happy with one of these book covers when it showed up. We knew from the beginning that we could expect to see great art, in exactly the style we were looking for. We had seen Sean Harrington's stuff online, and had asked him to do the cover for 'Zombie Zero: The First Zombie', as soon as he got back to us.

I had a good idea of what I wanted for that, and 'The Last Zombie'. The other six covers are all Sean Harrington's unique concepts. I sent him synopses of the stories, and he came up with ideas and turned them into the perfect art for each cover.

Like I said, we were never concerned that we wouldn't like what was coming. What we ended up being was incredibly excited, as we waited in eager anticipation for the next piece to show up. There were many talks about how cool each one that we had was, and how nice the prints were looking on our wall, and what might be the subject of the next cover.

The first three short story covers were all simply perfect. 'The Sickness Spreads' was a brilliant concept, brilliantly executed. 'The Beginning of the End' may not have been the most original title, but it was a beautifully original cover. We got to see how seriously badass a certain general looked through the eyes of the artist with that one, and how spooky these monsters could be. The third volume, 'Love Lost at Sea', was exactly the kind of eye-catching art that I used to expect from old pulp horror publications, in a startling and wonderful fashion.

Yet again, this cover stunned us in a whole new way when it arrived. The characters in these stories are incredibly formidable as warriors, and that's part of what attracted me to writing them. The other part was the amazing vulnerability that these folks kept carefully hidden under their toughness, and the intense bonds they had formed with each other. Somehow the cover that arrived conveyed both that hardness and that vulnerability, and I couldn't be more proud to have it on the front of this book.

Have another look, if you want. I'll wait. Come back to this spot when you're done, though, if you would; I'd like to tell you a little about my partner in all things.

ODE TO DAWN MARSHALL

A few years ago, I became part of a 'we'. Her name is Dawn, the other part of my precious 'we'; and she plays a big role in every part of my life. I often call her my 'partner in all things', and it's a pretty apt description. Besides giving me a peaceful and happy love life, she has also gone to great lengths to make my dreams come true. The library of books that I have written has gone from one to many due to her hard work and dedication, and it just keeps on growing.

There's a lot I could say here about the technical and professional skills that Dawn brought to the table or developed these last few years, but I'd like to take this in a slightly different direction instead. Those abilities are considerable, and invaluable; but they wouldn't do either of us much good if she hadn't been instrumental in making something other than my library grow.

My heart was in need of some serious overhaul work when it fell into Dawn's hands, and somehow she seemed to know instinctively how to care for it.

There were a few bumps in the road, there in the beginning, that were clearly me standing in the way of both us and myself. With the help of the love she was pouring into my heart, it grew; and I like to think I did too. One of the things that definitely happened was that my mind cleared up in ways it never had before.

This heart happiness brought on a whole new wave of creativity for me, taking me to a place where I felt as though the elusive muse had become my constant companion. It was perfect timing, since we were figuring out an aggressive publishing schedule to complement our ability to work together seamlessly. The ideas flooded my head, and keep on flooding it like never before, and I know I have Dawn to thank for that.

By extension, I have someone else to thank. Dawn brought along what I at first mistook for furry baggage, in the form of a giant dog named Mammoth. We tolerated each other for a minute; then we started to spend a little more time together; then we became the best of buddies. I still maintain that I am not a dog person. One of my favorite beings happens to be of the canine persuasion, that's all. Or so it was...

I guess Ximena makes two.

ABOUT JULIA'S FAMILY

By the time this set of stories began to take shape, all of them were outlined and ready to go. For the most part, I had everything either written or laid out to be written when I got to this set. What I didn't have was a good idea of which order the sets should be released, or which order the stories should all go in the sets. This was a time to let the stories speak to me, and for me to listen carefully as they did.

One of the very cool aspects of working on this project was having the ability to jump around within the project. Sometimes I get stuck in a story, and that can be a little frustrating when I'm writing a full-length novel. (Just kidding; it's maddening.)

That was not the case with these stories. If one got stalled, I could easily jump to another. At first it seemed random; then a pattern began to take shape. Part of that pattern was the stories speaking to me, telling me what order everything needed to fall in; nowhere was that ordered communication more clear than in this set.

I started on what I thought was the first of these stories, then worked on the tie-in between it and what I thought would be one of the last stories, then started this one. Without going back to any other story, I wrote this one straight through. Having started it after beginning fourteen other stories, and having finished twelve of those, I began this as the fifteenth and finished it thirteenth. (Whoa, that's a lot of numbers.)

As soon as I met Julia, I knew her story would be first. She has the stark vulnerability that I seriously admire in a truly formidable person. The things that happened to her in the past, the battle she is now fighting, and the steely righteousness of her perspective all appealed to me and my love of the deeper meaning. The fact that this type of person is not someone we ordinarily get to meet, or get to know this well, appealed to me even more. Peeking into Julia's mind with intense curiosity and sincere admiration showed me things I couldn't have otherwise seen so clearly, and it was easy to stick with this story until it was done.

I hope you love Julia's unique attitude, her true toughness, and her indomitable determination; I know I did.

Most of all, I hope you love 'Julia's Family'.

JULIA'S FAMILY

"Zee Kay three-two-seven, do you have the location?"

Julia was so lost in thought that the voice didn't register at first; she finished stuffing her bag and zipping it closed before she looked up, and over at him.

"I've got it, Zee Kay three-three-zero," she nodded. "You driving?"

"Yup." He took off his helmet, grinned at her. "You ready?"

"Always, Smiley," she nodded. "Put your helmet back on."

His face was still grinning when he pulled the steel covering over it. Julia moved to the door, waited for the others to stand at attention before opening it. As they finished getting ready, he came to stand bedside her. He was still smiling; she could hear it in his voice.

"We're going to see some real action," he said, nudging her. "Aren't you excited?"

Julia turned to him, slowly.

"This is just a training exercise," she replied flatly.

"And then?"Smiley shrugged. "If we're training military personnel, then that means there's been an outbreak. A real one."

Julia shook her head, heard the moving seam between her body armor and her helmet scrape with the motion. The armor was incredible, the best version she had ever seen when it came to preventing damage; but it was noisy.

"There has not been an outbreak," Julia said, loud enough for them all to hear. "This is a purely precautionary measure."

None of them said anything; if she was reading their body language right, a couple of them relaxed. A few helmets tipped forward, almost imperceptibly, and one of them crossed himself quickly; but no one spoke.

Smiley nudged her again.

"You don't want to see some action?" He was still smiling, under his mask. Julia was glad she couldn't see it; it was annoying her just hearing it. If she was continuing to read them right, the troops were annoyed as well. She wished she hadn't given him the moniker, briefly.

"No," Julia snapped, making sure it was a little harsh. "None if us want to see action. If this unit sees action it means everyone you love is dead or dying or eating someone else you love. I know you are the newest member of this team, but I was under the impression that you know what we are training for."

"He hasn't been on a red operation yet," one of the troops reminded her. "He's never even seen one."

"I've watched the videos," Smiley retorted. He wasn't smiling any more. "I was a ranger. I headed up twenty-two successful missions."

"Which is what got you in the door," Julia nodded. "To step one. Did you see my first red operation? The video?"

They were starting to line up behind her, prepared for three days in another secret facility in less than ten minutes. Another spoke, the one the government knew as Zee Kay three-one-seven. She called him 'Blunt'.

"They don't show that video to new recruits," he said. "It freaks them out. I was there; I still have nightmares."

She nodded. Julia led the team in tactical operations; she had her own way of naming those that served under her. She chose her favorite quality about them, and called them that.

"What happened?" His smile was definitely gone now.

"As you know, a red operation is very dangerous." They gathered closer as she spoke, clearing wanting to hear. Many of them remembered the event, those that had been there; they had all heard about it. None of them had never heard her tell the story.

"They take a select number of death row inmates or political prisoners and turn them," she went on. "They know how many, but they don't tell us. We find out in the red room. You know how many places there are to hide in there, even in full light. Well, they dim it down, or make it dark, and send us in one at a time. Newbies always go last, Smiley, or they're supposed to. But I was like you. I'd been training to be a zombie killer for months; I was ready to be a zombie killer for real. I pushed my way to the front, and went in first."

They were all ready; they were all listening. Julia knew they should get moving; she also knew that three days was not enough time to train even the most special forces. She continued.

"I bumped into a rambler right away," she said. "It caught me by surprise, and pulled me to the floor with it. It was so strong, and determined. It was biting at me right away, and I couldn't get it off me. The armor was different then, and it crumpled and came apart. It cut me, the armor, and as soon as I felt the blood I heard the first howl."

Julia shuddered, remembering.

"I knew it would be two minutes before the next team member came in; those are the rules of a red operation, no matter what." Julia sighed. "But I panicked, and froze, when I saw the howler coming. It was so fast, and so big; I never even got a shot off. It batted the rambler off me, and went right for my exposed flesh. It bit me."

Smiley gasped.

"Bullshit," he breathed.

Julia laughed humorlessly.

"How many of you have been bitten?" she asked.

Four hands went up quickly; then a fifth, slowly. Their armor clanked noisily with the movement. Smiley looked them over, as their hands fell to their sides again.

"Bullshit," he repeated. It was quiet this time, breathless.

"I got bit and turned into a mindless starving drone," Blunt said. "Not her, though. Tell him, Captain; tell him what you did."

"We need to go," Julia insisted.

Now it was a chorus of voices. They were

usually quiet, as individuals and as a group. The small personal concession Julia had made had opened that door a crack; their protestations were slipping through it.

Julia shrugged. They all knew the truth she knew, except perhaps Smiley; either this was a false alarm, or they were all dead anyway.

"I turned into a monster, and lost it," she shrugged again.

The chorus of voices booed; Blunt leaned forward.

"That's not the whole truth, Chief," he said. "That's what happened to me, maybe; I don't remember anything after I got bit, except hunger. They told me after; I just wandered around trying to eat my teammates. But that's not what happened when you turned."

The team put their attention on Blunt; Julia was glad for it. She had made the point she wanted to make. The rest of the story was as much a blur to her as it was a legend to them.

"She tossed the howler off her somehow, and went for the rambler," Blunt took up the story, as they turned toward him. "Before the first two minutes were up, she had eaten the rambler and changed again. When we started to come in, she was hunting down the howlers one by one."

Blunt glanced at her, to make sure it was okay for him to talk about this. Julia nodded, slightly. She frowned behind her mask.

"The strategy is generally the same when we enter the red room," Blunt explained. "Each of us finds a defensible position, and posts up until the rest of the team comes in. We followed the strategy this time, but all we did was watch. There were no attacks on us, and no time for us to advance once we had all made it into position. The only thing left alive in the room was us and her; she wouldn't attack us, and we made no aggressive action against her. We swept the area, counted the bodies and formed a defensive circle around her until they brought in a treatment unit. We stayed with her in the red room until she had changed back. Then we nominated her to be our tactical chief whenever we are in the field. We would have all stepped down if they had refused."

Smiley turned to her, and Julia shrugged. "Let's go," she said.

* * *

Julia hated public speaking of any kind.

The team was her family, the only one she had ever cared for; everyone else was on the outside, and not invited to look in. It may have been a strange thing for someone else, sharing such a huge secret and responsibility with so few others; for Julia, it was natural. She gained her strength from the iron bonds that linked them, the knowledge that they shared and the burden that they shouldered. She was happy to have her helmet on when she addressed the assembled troops. She was also glad to see that the General was among them.

It all made sense to her now. General Roberts was a name she had heard many times, first when she had been thrust into a leadership role and then when she had started seeing Leo. Though she had never met him, he was her point of contact if anything happened to Leo. Julia had honestly hoped to never see the man's face; she was surprised to see gentleness in it, and the advanced signs of aging. She had always thought of him as Leo's age, or a little older; it made her sad to think that he had nearly made it to the end without being called upon.

"I won't mince words," she said, looking at the General and knowing that no one could see her eyes. "We are a specialized unit. We are trained to handle one specific threat, and that threat is becoming a reality. There are not enough of us. We will be training you for the next few days, teaching you to better handle this threat. I requested a special demonstration, and your commander has been good enough to agree to provide what I needed. Please put your attention on the north entrance, and do try not to scream."

There was uneasy laughter, and the sound of several hundred bodies turning. It was followed by a few involuntary cries, and a whispered sea of hushed murmuring. The creature was held by chains, the links held taut by her armored comrades, and it captured their attention completely. They did not turn back, even when she spoke again. That suited Julia just fine.

"We are zombie killers," she went on. "Twenty years ago, an outbreak was prevented by your commander. He was working with my commander. They are the only ones that lived to tell the tale, and it's not easy to get either of them to talk about it."

One person laughed at that; the rest were still staring at the monster that had appeared among them. Julia inclined her helmet in the

General's direction, and he chuckled again.

"If that thing bites you, you change," she said. "You lose your mind to a hunger for human flesh, while your own flesh rots from your body. If you feed, you become like that thing. All that thing wants to do is feed, and all it wants to feed on is flesh. It is as smart as a human, as fast as a wildcat and as strong as a bear. Its bones are nearly unbreakable, and it heals rapidly from nearly any wound. Any questions?"

"How do you kill it?"

She didn't see the person that asked; she didn't have to.

"Good question," Julia nodded. "And the only one that matters. You have to sever its head fully from its body, or destroy the creature completely. If you are a very steady sharpshooter, a bullet placed properly in the eye will do it as well; if not, don't even try. You're more likely to hit yourself with a ricochet than kill one of these things shooting it in the head. Any other questions?"

"When do we start?"

She saw the speaker that time; it was the same voice, a giant of a man with his automatic rifle at the ready.

"Right now," Julia said. She smiled at him, although she knew he couldn't see it through her mask. She waved her hand, and her team members moved as one. They dropped the chains, stepped back and drew their swords. The thing eyed them, as they continued to back away; it turned as a few people cried out again. Everyone moved away slowly while it watched; all but the giant of a man who had spoken. He dropped to one knee, aimed his rifle and called out.

"Get back!" he cried. "Clear! I'm taking the shot!"

Gunfire erupted, echoing through the tall chamber. Julia spoke. She didn't bother raising her voice; he wouldn't hear.

"You're just pissing it off," she muttered.

It was true; the monster turned away from the volley of bullets; they tore through its arms and legs and torso; the wounds healed before they could trickle blood. When the clip was exhausted, the monster turned to its attacker and howled. The man dropped the weapon, and the clip he had been fumbling with; his eyes went wide, and his hands began to tremble. All the while the monster moved toward him, a lightning blur that noisily trailed chains and crossed the space between them in a heartbeat. His head cracked on the concrete as it leapt on top of him, taking him to the floor. The monster reared back, opened its cavernous mouth and snapped at his face.

Julia took up one of the chains and yanked with all of her augmented might. The cluttered space had become an open floor, and she let the thing fly past her. She tugged the chain again as it reached the end, and the monster crumpled to the floor. It writhed, leapt to its feet and came at her. Julia let it hit her full in the chest, tossed it as her back hit the hard concrete, and stood again with the momentum of the swinging chain. The monster picked up one of the other trailing series of links as it gained its footing once more; it swung it, and tossed the chain at her head.

She fell backward, glad for the way the helmet cushioned both blows; as her head struck the hard floor, her wrist cannon let out a soft whooshing sound. The blow didn't jar her skull, but it jarred her vision; she had to roll and stand to see what damage she had done.

It was perfect, just what she had been hoping for. The monster's right forearm was gone, exploded into a mess of gore that dangled limply from its elbow. She heard a gasp as the gathered troops watched; the thing's arm was growing back, right before their eyes. It lost a little mass, and gained a new forearm, all in the space of a few seconds.

Julia drew her sword.

"We don't have wrist cannons for all of you," she said. "We don't have the time or the resources to get you all specially fitted armor like ours. But we do have some swords for you."

She waved it in the air; the monster watched her, and the bluish blade.

"These are no ordinary swords," she continued. "They are sharp and strong like nothing you have ever seen. At soon as this monster's hunger gets to be too much, I'll show you."

It looked at her, bemused hatred in its rusted red eyes.

"It can't see my heat signature quite so well through the suit, and it can't smell my flesh either." She waved the sword, and laughed. "It knows that I'm in here, though, make no mistake; that ugly creature wants to rip open this suit and sink hungry teeth into my-"

It was so fast, when it moved. By the time anyone could gasp or shout, it was upon her again. Julia speared it through the middle, and regretted it immediately. Her sword was trapped between them, and the thing was biting at her face. Its jaws cranked maniacally, breaking teeth on the one-way visor. Julia could see the rows of jagged biters as it worked at the mask. She heard a voice in her ear, and frowned at the sound of it.

"Need help, Chief?"

"Don't you dare, Dancer," she snapped. "They need to see this."

Suddenly she was in the air, the sword coming free. The monster had grabbed her, and tossed her like a rag doll. Julia twisted her body, angled her sword as best she could, and speared it through the neck as it blurred across the space between them to leap at her again. She felt it come down on her chest plate with all of its weight and might, and she heard the low creak of metal as the breath whooshed out of her body. She twisted the blade as it pounded at her again, and held her breath as its eyes rolled back in its head.

It took everything she had to mount it, and pull the blade free. The first swing was awkwardly intercepted by its shoulder as the creature swung at her; Julia hit the floor, rolled to her feet and attacked again.

The next swing caught it full in the face.

Part of the monster's jaw fell to the floor, all teeth and exposed sinew. It staggered, and she swung again; the sword sunk into the creature's neck, lodging stubbornly in its spine. Julia cried out, and yanked the blade free; the creature followed, downing her once more. The dent in her armor dug painfully into Julia's ribs. It chomped at her face again, and all she could see for a few disgusting moments were white spots and teeth and a damaged monster jaw growing back up close; her upward slices finally found purchase, and the monster rolled off her with a pained howl.

It was on its knees, losing mass as it tried to grow back another arm. Julia advanced, swung the blade; the monster put up its other arm, and it was sliced off at the wrist. The blade bit deep into its neck once more, and the monster went limp. She yanked the sword free, swinging again before the life could come back into its eyes. The monster's head hung from a last grisly string of flesh, and her next swing cleaved easily through it.

Julia collapsed to the floor beside the monster, and clawed at the seams of her armor. She peeled it off piece by piece, the breastplate and backplate coming loose at once. Gasping for breath, Julia slipped her fingers down to release the fastenings on her leggings. They fell away noisily; she stood in her bra and panties, helmet and boots. There was a scratch across her visor, a long tooth mark. Her torso was already bruising, a wide swath of painful purple stretching across her slim belly.

She was still gasping for breath when she began speaking.

"This armor is designed for battle with these things," she huffed. "Our weapons are all developed to fight them."

Julia looked down at the twisted remains of her protective exoskeleton. She kicked at the lifeless head at her feet. It rolled toward some of the troops that had begun to gather in close as she started speaking; they backed away together.

"It's not enough," she spat. "One of us against one of them might get these kind of results, what some would call victory. But I am exposed now; if I had left the armor on, I would be unable to fight another howler. There are ten of us here, and two more of us back at our base. Individually we are more effective than a score of ground troops, yet we fall easily before this threat if we stand alone. It is only together that we stand a chance. My team functions as a single unit.

Our mind is one mind. Our purpose is a shared one, and without each other we are each nearly nothing."

Julia was tired of staring through the scratched visor. She thumbed the release, threw her helmet to the floor. A murmur went through the gathering, and Julia remembered: she was beautiful, and it affected people. She frowned, wishing she'd left it on.

"We are not here to teach you to fight," she continued. "You know how to fight. We are here to teach you to think as one unit, to act as the trained body of the mind that leads you. You all have great respect for the General, I can see that already. We will show you how to act at his thought rather than wait for a command; we will teach you to be an extension of the man who saved the world the first time these monsters appeared. And maybe then humanity will stand a chance."

There was a lot of tension in the giant room at this point. Julia had painted it on in layers, from her first words to the appearance of the monster; the battle had been easier than she had anticipated, but her nearly naked appearance after had completed the effect. Between revealing most of her skin and the finale of her face, the impression she had been trying to make had been made; it didn't matter how she had gotten there, only that she had. She turned to the General, stood to attention and saluted him smartly.

One lone voice called out, in defiant agreement. The tension broke, and a cheer went up, as their eyes met. The General saluted her back, and blinked away the tears in his eyes before anyone but her made note. They held each other's gaze, and the salute, while the voices boiled over into a shouted soup of sound.

Julia let her hand fall to her side, and let her gaze drop to the floor. She took a step, kicked the monster's head again, turned and strode for the door. The General's troops parted, and hers fell in behind her. Julia stopped on the other side of the door, and reached down to check her ribs. She winced as her fingers dug into her own tender torso.

"Looks painful, Chief," Smiley said. His voice was unusually somber.

"This feels one way," Julia touched the spot again, and smiled. She let her hand drift to her heart.

"This feels another," she said. "That is the way of life. So long as I feel, I live. This is life right here."

She balled her fist, struck her own

bruised rib, winced again. Julia put her hand on his armored shoulder, and smiled.

"One does not exist without the other," she murmured, still smiling.

"You are one seriously badass bitch, boss," he breathed. His smile was back; she could hear it in his voice. She let hers fall.

"With all due respect, Chief." He nodded. "What about your suit?"

"She got a new one this morning," Blunt said. "That's why she let that thing tear the old one to shreds. She's not just a badass, Smiley; she's the mind that she talked about out there, for us. The Chief is our only hope if there is an outbreak. Let her thoughts be your own. Don't question them; she already has, at length. If you don't jump higher than you've ever jumped when she asks for it, you fail us all; but worse, you fail her. That will not be tolerated, by any of us."

Smiley nodded. "I think I get it."

"You better," Blunt responded evenly.

"Enough," Julia said. "Go to the vehicle, get my other suit and the weapons we brought. The General will be sending our first batch of trainees into the yard; I will go meet with him and set up a training schedule. I have high hopes that we will be conducting red operations on a regular basis, given the General's initial cooperation. Bring the weapons into the yard; we will meet you there."

"Ah, Chief," Blunt nodded down at her near nakedness.

Julia sighed.

"Well, hell," she said. "Alright, let's get moving."

*   *   *

She found the General in his office; they had both changed, and wore similar fatigues. Julia noted the giant pistol hanging from his belt with a nod.

"Is that it?" she asked.

The General patted his hip, returned her nod. When she continued to gaze at the ordinary hunk of metal like it had some magical quality, he unclasped it and pulled the handgun from its holster. The General reversed it, held it out to her.

Julia ran her fingers over the handle, with the tender touch of a lover. She didn't take it; her hand fell to her side, and he slipped it back in the holster.

"We have limited time, sir," Julia said. "We can train your people in shifts, so they can eat and sleep and perform their duties.

My people do not need to take a break during this time. The quarters you have provided us are remarkably generous, and secure. I would turn the space into a red room; if you will consent and assist, sir."

"A red room," the General repeated. It didn't sound like a question; Julia answered it anyway.

"A space filled with ramblers and howlers alike," she said. "There is no more effective way to teach people to deal with this threat than to have them encounter the threat itself. The shock of seeing one of these creatures for the first time can be paralyzing. In that moment all the training in the world is just a waste of time, because that moment is all a howler needs. We need to make the sight of these monsters as routine to your people as lacing up their boots. We need a red room."

"Then you'll have one," the General nodded. "I don't see a reason to drive your unit so hard in training mine. The world may need you soon; I do not want to be the reason you are not rested or fed."

"We are trained to operate at peak performance for over a week without food or sleep," Julia pointed out. "Our purpose is to start fighting when the threat appears, and to not stop until the threat is put down.

With all due respect, sir, we will sleep when the last zombie is dead."

The General frowned; there was a hint of a smile in his eyes.

"Surely you see my point," he insisted. "I would have you consider a compromise."

Julia's shoulders went tense; she opened her mouth to reply. Remembering her orders, specifically, she held her tongue. She imagined her commander there before her, telling her to consider a compromise.

"Of course, sir," she nodded. "If you give us a single bunk and a single locker in your common sleeping quarters, I will make sure every member of my team sleeps two hours each day we are here."

"Including you?" The General arched an eyebrow at her.

"If those are your orders, sir, I will follow them."

"They are," he nodded. "I need your help, but the world needs it more than I do. Eat and sleep and train my troops; when you leave here, I want you fresh and ready for battle. Do you understand?"

"I understand, sir."

The General sighed. "Do you think we stand a chance?"

Julia shook her head, almost imperceptibly.

"No, sir," she replied flatly. "Do you?"

"Of course not," he muttered. "I may be old, but I am not an old fool."

They considered their own thoughts, quietly, briefly.

"Have you given up, sir?" Julia asked.

The General cocked an eyebrow at her.

"Of course not," he smiled. "And neither have you. Isn't that right?"

"Yes, sir," she nodded. "Now, about that red room. How many prisoners does this facility currently house?"

* * *

The days went by quickly although she was painfully present in every moment. Julia watched the General's troops become galvanized by the threat they faced together. She saw personal bonds forming between her people and his, and allowed for it. Smiley had become her champion somewhere between hearing her story and starting the training. He began nearly every sentence with "The chief says...", and he almost never smiled anymore. Blunt and Silent both lived up to their names, and made it clear that they weren't here to make friends; but Style and Quick took young soldiers under their wings, and Dancer was clearly falling for one of the young men he was working with. They only wore their suits when leading people into the red room, and only stepped in when necessary. There were a few scratches, but no bites.

She floated between groups, as the General did the same. Julia nearly asked him if he was sleeping or eating, as he had ordered her to; but she never saw him when one of his subordinates or hers were not around again, and never got the chance. He seemed as pleased to let folks get close as her, or not displeased enough to prevent it. Rather than get in the way, the camaraderie helped the training go faster and take hold more firmly. Julia felt something begin within her as she watched them, and worked with them; it had grown and solidified within her. On the last day she gathered them again; she wore her new suit, and held her sword in her hand while she addressed them. The fluorescents glinted off the bluish blade as she swung it to make her points.

"When we arrived here," she called out, "one howler could have taken this entire compound."

There were nods in the crowd, murmurs of assent; they had all been in the red room.

"Now," Julia cried, "Half of you could turn, and the other half would put them down. You have stepped up these past few days, and elevated yourselves to the most elite rank of soldier there is. You are zombie killers, each and every one of you. If it were up to me, I would take this entire assemblage as my team. I would step confidently into a sea of these monsters with this incredible group of warriors at my back. If this threat passes, for whatever reason, your General and I will disagree for the first time, and we will spend the rest of our careers fighting over this fine batch of fighters I see before me."

They cheered, until they realized that the General was speaking; then the collective outcry died suddenly, and there was no sound but his voice.

"In the meantime," he said. "There is much work to do. You have five minutes. Say your goodbyes, and let these people get back to their jobs."

The General stood back on one side of the room, Julia on the other. Every member of her unit went to him, saluted the General and exchanged a few words. Julia watched the interactions between the similar exchanges she had with members of his team. Julia was not accustomed to having her abilities be known by so many, or appreciated so openly; she was glad for her mask every time she flushed. When her internal clock was arriving at five minutes, she turned to step toward him. As she looked up, she saw the General watching her; there were tears in his eyes again, but only for as long as it took for him to blink them away. Rather than approach her, he stood at stiff attention where he was. He saluted her from across the room, and held the rigid pose.

Julia sheathed her sword, and lifted her eyes to meet his through the one-way visor. In the seconds it took her to look down, they all joined him in his standing salute. For a moment she was shocked still; keeping her greatness secret had been a part of her life all of her life. It was a jarring surprise to see them all standing at attention, saluting; many of them were smiling, and more than one set of eyes were shining bright with tears.

Lifting her hands, Julia unclasped the helmet and lifted it over her head. She let them see her own smile, and her tears. Tucking the helmet under her elbow, she lifted her hand slowly to salute them in return. When her hand touched her forehead lightly, a single exclamation became a deafening roar of triumphant cries before the first sound had died. The collective battle cry shook the walls, and set Julia's ribs to trembling inside her exoskeleton armor.

She placed the helmet back in its place, turned smartly and strode from the room. Her team followed Julia out of the safety of the locked down facility and into a world that was already beginning to fall apart.

ABOUT LISA'S LIST

Julia showed me a bunch of things, and I was grateful to her for the sacred peek into her innermost thoughts. She also showed me what order these three stories needed to be released in, and I was glad for that too. Although I had started what was to be the last one first, I saw what needed to come next as soon as I finished telling Julia's story. Rather than jump forward and back to the last story, I did the same thing with the next one that I had done with 'Julia's Family'.

'Lisa's List' was therefore started sixteenth, and written straight through to be completed fourteenth. It took me deeper into the lives of these warriors than I had expected to go, and showed me even more of their personal depths than I had anticipated. Lisa was brought up to live in shame, but somehow she discovered the beautiful aspects of embracing pride despite her programming. She is the emotional glue that helps hold this unit together more tightly than ever, while being as much a badass as any of the others.

These people are not soft, in any sense of the word. What some might consider them showing their softer side was actually them revealing the foundation of their formidability. It was a special thing to be shown, and to be able to share with you.

That last story tied in to 'Zombie Zero: The First Zombie' in a somewhat indirect manner. You see Julia, in the italicized section at the beginning of Chapter Fourteen; but she's with the others, and suited up, and you might not have recognized her individually. I didn't think the tie-in was strong enough to mention, until now.

Lisa's story also ties in to the beginning of Chapter Fourteen; but that's not all. It ties in with the dramatic end of that same chapter, and again with the events that take place in Chapter Seventeen. Of course, it also ties into that last short story; and the next one.

All you need to do in order to get the point of this whole story is read the rest of this book. If you want to know how it ties in to the main story, you might want to read 'Zombie Zero: The First Zombie'.

If you have already read that book, first of all: thank you! Second, I hope you love reading this tie-in as much as I loved writing it. Really, I hope everyone loves 'Lisa's List'.

LISA'S LIST

"You know that every new recruit thinks that you don't have a heart," Lisa said. "It's not hard to see why, when you talk like that."

He curbed the wheels, slid the arm on the steering column until it stopped, and turned off the ignition. Leo left the keys in it. Still looking ahead, sitting unmoving for a moment, he shrugged.

"I don't care what new recruits think of me," he said. "I don't care what anyone thinks of me except the people I think of."

She nodded. "And we all think you have an oversized heart. It's why you never smile, or frown; if you let the expressions start flowing, they'd never stop. You would spend all day hugging us and telling us all how proud you are of us, and we wouldn't get any training done. So you keep it locked inside, and let it drive you even harder."

He turned his head slowly, to meet her eyes. There was still no hint of an expression on his face.

"Is that right?" he asked.

She smirked. "Am I wrong?"

Suddenly there was a softness in his eyes; he leaned forward, and brushed his lips against hers. He noted her shocked expression, while his remained serene.

"I love you, Lisa," Leo said.

It was the most beautiful and terrifying moment of her entire day. Suddenly it hit home for Lisa; he thought they would be dead soon. He thought that everyone would be dead soon. This wasn't training, or a drill; this was an actual outbreak. She shuddered as he got out of the car; she shook it off, and followed.

"Hey!" Someone in a uniform was yelling at Leo; he was ignoring the voice, heading for the revolving glass.

"Hey!" The man caught up to him, grabbed Leo by the arm. "You can't park there!"

Lisa couldn't explain; it had to be the sudden shock of the truth hitting home, or Leo's uncharacteristic behavior that made her do it. She reached for her handgun, automatically, ready to put him down the moment his hand fell on her commander. Lisa felt Leo move between them, and conceal the weapon from view; he pulled out one of his badges while she collected herself, and holstered the pistol again.

"I actually can park there," Leo said calmly. "I am a special agent of the CDC, and there is a very dangerous person in your airport. I can take the extra minutes to park, killing thousands, or I can go stop her."

He shoved the identification in the man's face, glanced at the man's badge.

"You may want the deaths of thousands of people on your hands, agent Morris, but I don't," Leo added. "I don't have time to work this out with you, and you're not adequately trained to stop me. Do whatever you want."

Leo turned, and strode off; it gave the man a moment to glimpse Lisa's weapon, and the look in her eye that suggested that she would not hesitate to use it. He backed off.

"I'll keep an eye on it for you, Special Agent," he called out as the door revolved them into the airport.

With a glance at the board, Leo started walking.

"They've already landed," he said, as she fell into step beside him. "Let's head to the baggage claim. Would you hack into the airport security cameras, see if you can spot her coming off the plane or down the hall? Look for the people near her, see if they show any signs."

Lisa scrolled through screens, typed in codes and fast forwarded through video feeds. She nudged him as the rotating metal sheets came into view.

"She looks awful," Lisa said. "See? It looks like a young lady, college aged, that died three days ago. Almost all the flesh is gone from her face already."

Leo stopped, looked closer. "See that woman, behind her? Tell me that isn't the same woman standing over there."

Lisa glanced over, nodded.

"It is," she said. "I don't see the girl, though."

He talked over his shoulder as he walked.

"If she's that far gone," he said, "she wouldn't have stopped for luggage. She would have been consumed by her hunger. I can't believe she made it off the plane without biting anyone."

"Zee Kay zero-zero-one, hold up." Lisa's hand on his arm halted him; they both watched the woman while she spoke in hushed tones.

"She looks sick," Lisa murmured. "And do you see that other woman, looking at her? She looks even worse."

Leo nodded, leaned in closer.

"I see," he said. "I don't think either of

them is advanced enough to try to bite us, but they look like they're moving pretty slow. We should have time to get them both."

"Really?" Lisa breathed. "You think they're infected?"

Leo pulled his arm away, spoke as he moved toward the ashen woman again.

"I think we should treat them as though they are," he said.

She followed, blocked the woman's escape while Leo addressed her.

"Excuse me, ma'am," he said. "We're going to have to ask you to come with us."

Lisa was not shy about letting her hand drift to her weapon. The woman watched Lisa's movement, her eyes going wide. She laughed, and started coughing uncontrollably. Sputtering, she shook her head. She laughed again.

"I'm sorry," she said. "You must have me confused with someone else."

Leo glanced at her, perhaps expecting a mush-mouthed moan instead of coherent speech; he shook his head firmly.

"Please," he repeated. "Come with us."

Leo walked in step with both women, a safe stride behind the suspect. He watched Lisa map out the airport on her device while he spoke calmly to the woman; soon they were at a door marked 'Security Personnel Only' with a keypad next to the handle. Lisa flashed the code at him on her device, and Leo punched it in. The room was perfect, with an empty cell in the corner. The woman was a little resistant to the idea, but they got her quickly contained and went after the other one.

She was in much worse condition, and tried harder to resist being taken into custody. Leo was glad when they dropped them off at the hospital, and notified the proper channels where to find them. County would be flooded with some of the finest military doctors and scientists over the next few hours, and very few people would know. It was a relief to know that they could finally bring all the minds that might solve this problem to bear on it at last. The cure they had developed with their limited resources took too long, to make and to work.

He glanced over at Lisa, after they had driven a couple blocks; the relief was visible on her face as well.

"Can we track the other one?" she asked.

"We can try," he responded. "The machine that picks up the signature is not portable, but we can monitor it when we get back to base. Our tracking will basically follow her around, but it won't be in real time. We will have to wait until she stops moving to close in on her."

Lisa shuddered. "And what if she bites someone?"

"Then it's too late anyway." Leo watched the road, kept his speed steady and his countenance clear. "For all of us."

He glanced over again.

"Be hopeful," he said, as his eyes found the road once more. "She could have fed on the plane if she wanted to, or at the airport. She didn't; maybe she isn't consumed by it."

"You mean like Julia, when she got bit?"

Leo nodded. "You weren't there for that. It was amazing."

"She's pretty amazing all around," Lisa smiled. "What's really amazing is that you've never been bitten. You ran security at a facility that researched them, didn't you?"

"Where did you hear that?" Leo shook his head. "I swear, 'classified' has lost its meaning."

Lisa laughed. "Word gets around, especially in a unit like ours. I heard that only you and one other person survived the shutdown. How long was the facility active?"

"It's still active," he shrugged. "They scrubbed all the blood clean, turned it into a top secret political prison and research facility, and put the only other survivor of the shutdown in charge of the place. He has more troops; we have more training, and weapons specifically designed to battle this threat. At a time like this, we are to come together and combine our resources to deal with whatever we need to deal with. It's where the rest of the unit went, to train his people."

Lisa watched him drive for a few silent moments. She pulled her device from her pocket, started swiping screens aside and tapping the lighted face.

"What are you doing?" Leo asked, glancing over.

Lisa kept tapping and swiping. "I'm going to find that girl. We're going to put an end to the end of the world."

* * *

"Lisa, I wish you would tell us what's going on."

Her mother frowned sternly at her; Lisa's father stood over her mother's shoulder, wearing the same sober expression. His glasses were perched on the end of his nose; otherwise they looked like nearly the same person. They had shared the same set of facial expressions for so long that it appeared as though they now shared the same set of features as well.

Lisa had been ordered to come here; it was the only reason she stood in the uncomfortably familiar space, trying not to breathe in the dense atmosphere. She met her mother's glassy eyes.

Lisa sighed. "What are you talking about?"

"You know what she's talking about," her father frowned. "Your whole life has been nothing but secrets since you left home. We see you once a year, maybe twice, and you won't talk about anything."

"My work is top secret," Lisa shrugged, "and you wouldn't approve of my love life. There's not much else to talk about."

"Oh, dear," her mother tsked. "There's a lot more to talk about than government work and social impropriety. Can't you stay for awhile this time? Maybe come to services on Sunday?"

Lisa bit her lip, and her tongue.

"I just wanted to check in on you guys," she said. "Make sure you have everything you need."

"Of course we do," her father put his arm

around her mother. "We have each other, and we have the Lord. We do wish you would stay with us, come back to the path that calls you."

"This is the path that calls me," Lisa retorted hotly, before she could bite her tongue again. She saw a look of mild disgust cross her father's face; her mother turned into him, away from her.

"I'm helping people," Lisa went on. "I came here to help you. Have you been watching the news?"

Lisa watched her mother burrow her face deeper into her father's chest. His father glared at her, frowning fiercely.

"You mean the zombie prank?" he asked stiffly. "It's not funny. Your mother is very upset. I don't know how this generation gets away with treating the news like an entertainment forum."

"It's not a prank," Lisa shook her head. "There has been an outbreak in several countries, and it may be only a matter of time before there's one here. That's why I'm here, to get you somewhere safe."

Her mother cried out, and looked up at her father.

"We are as safe as we will ever be," he said, squeezing his wife's shoulders. "We are in God's hands."

"Can't you be in God's hands inside a safe house?" Lisa sputtered, exasperated. She took a half step toward them, reached out with one hand tentatively. Her father backed away, clutching her mother to him.

"If what you are saying is true, it is God's plan," her father said stiffly. "Stay here with us, make your peace and unburden your sins. We will all be called home one day; perhaps this is the day. Perhaps you did not come here to save us. Have you considered that you came here for another reason? A reason you don't wish to admit to yourself?"

Her mother came back to life, turning toward Lisa with tears in her eyes and a beatific smile on her face.

"Of course," she breathed. "You came here so we could save you."

Lisa shook her head. She felt her hands ball into fists.

"This isn't the rapture, you fools," she scoffed. "It's a goddamned zombie apocalypse."

Her mother gasped, and buried her head once more. Her father frowned, and shook his head sadly at her.

"I think you should go," he snapped.

"Finally," Lisa threw up her hands.

"Something we agree on."

She stormed out of the house, slamming the door behind her. Lisa swore under her breath down the entire walkway, while she got into the vehicle and long after she had driven off. At a stoplight just like all the other stoplights, she suddenly grew silent. Her breathing calmed, her shoulders relaxed, and her heart slowed.

It had gone exactly as she had expected; she didn't know why it had upset her. Lisa had lost her parents a long time ago, when she had first shown more than a friendly interest in another young girl. They had gone from dragging her to church once a year for Easter to insisting they all go every Sunday. Every sentence they spoke was about God or the church, or led back to it. There were no more movie nights or honest talks, just careful explanations about what God wanted for her. Her teenage years had been one long lesson in her own wickedness, and her freedom had only come with adulthood. Lisa almost couldn't remember the people they used to be, and how they used to treat her, before she had begun to become herself.

A smile grew on her face as she crossed town, thinking ahead to who she would be seeing next. They were the real members of her family, the husbands and wives and children of her teammates. Even those that had fallen had known their loved ones would not drift from the fold; the families mostly belonged to those that had been lost long ago. At least that's how the outside world saw it; to her, and to all of them, they were as much a part of the family now as when they had served. A loss for one of them was a loss for all of them; no one bore it alone.

She could talk to them; she could save them, at least for a little while. Lisa turned on the radio, switched from the news feed and listened to a pop song. She hummed along, smiling contentedly to herself.

Lisa hadn't given up on finding the girl; but her orders superseded her own desire, and Leo was doing the only thing that could be done. She was glad for the chance to say goodbye, and to maybe save some of them. Thinking back on it, she realized that she was glad she had stopped to see the people that used to be her family first. It put things in perspective, and galvanized her will to follow out her orders. Lisa would get them to safety, and answer their questions as best she could; then she would get on to the next item on her list.

She could see it in her mind, like always,

the picture perfect image of a lined sheet of paper. It had been filled with items a few days ago, items that would have been checked off within a week had she left them; nothing ever survived more than a few days on Lisa's list. All of those words had been cleared with one swipe of her mental eraser, to be replaced by four words in bold and underlined neat cursive.

END THE ZOMBIE APOCALYPSE.

There had to be a way. Lisa watched for it, from the corner of her mind, as she talked with them and hugged them and explained as best she could. There was always a way. She helped some of them pack, she carried luggage and children to vehicles and bunkers. No problem had ever been created that didn't have a solution; someone just had to find it. Lisa kept her smile up until they were all locked down, and kept a part of her mind constantly alert for clues.

It would have probably surprised her parents, to find that Lisa had her own brand of faith. It didn't surprise her; it was the inner knowing that had pulled her away from them in the first place, the same inner knowing that had propelled her down every path that meant anything to her. Lisa had watched people give up her whole life: first her parents, and then her competition. She had risen easily through the ranks for a variety of reasons; but if one single thing had elevated her to the status of zombie killer, it was her inability to give up. Nothing had ever survived its spot on her inner list of things to do; Lisa was damned if she was going to let the first time be zombies.

* * *

It all happened so fast. It seemed to her that one minute it was all coming together; they had brought in the girl, and had developed a pill that was working on all of their experimental patients. She was most interested in the girl, and the strange knowledge she seemed to have. Lisa spent all the time with her that she could, nursing her back to human and listening to her warnings. She encouraged the girl to eat, told her how much better she was looking, and even cheered when she finally kept a little yogurt down.

Then the tide turned, and in the next minute it seemed all would be lost. First were the reports of random outbreaks, followed by her and Leo's harrowing brush with death at the hospital. The worst of the news broke over the intercom, while she was talking with the patient and encouraging her to eat more. Lisa heard the general alert before her earpiece came to life, and she stood at the sound.

"Attention," the voice came over the loudspeaker in every room. "There has been an unauthorized and uncontrolled outbreak in the facility. Code red. All staff report to your red stations."

Her earpiece chattered.

"Zee Kay three-two-seven," a mechanical voice said in her ear. "Report to the ready room."

Lisa sat beside her again.

"Elayna, I need to go," she said. "If I can, I'll be back. I can't thank you enough for working with us, and sharing so much about your experience. I can't imagine how hard it must have been."

Elayna laughed quietly.

"Probably no harder than watching a monster become human again," she shrugged.

"You're no monster," Lisa reached for her hand; Elayna drew back.

"Don't touch me," Elayna gasped. "You could get infected."

Lisa shook her head.

"I've been inoculated," she said, taking her hand. "Because of you, and the women sitting with you on the flight, we have been able to work on this night and day. There is a cure, Elayna. There's hope."

Elayna smiled weakly. There didn't seem to be much hope in her eyes, or in the smile. She squeezed Lisa's hand.

"Thank you," she said. "Goodbye, Lisa."

Rising at her bedside once more, Lisa smiled down at her while Elayna's hand slipped from hers.

"This is not goodbye," Lisa assured her. "I am trained to battle this threat, and that is exactly what I am going to do. My team and I are going to take back control of this facility. Then we'll take back the country."

Elayna nodded. "And then the world."

"That's right."

"Goodbye, Lisa," Elayna repeated.

Lisa moved to the door, shaking her head. Swiping her badge across the reader, she sighed as the door clicked open.

"I'll be back," she said over her shoulder. "You'll see."

A hungry howl filled the air as she pulled the door shut behind her. Lisa made for the stairs, and leapt up the flights to the ready room. In less than five minutes the team was assembled, armored and ready for battle. She couldn't see Leo's face, but the calm in his voice helped steady her nerves. His orders were not what she had expected.

"We need to split up again," he told them. "Zee Kay three-two-seven and I will take back the facility; the rest of you need to take back the surrounding area. Stay close, and work together. You have all met General Roberts. His troops will be coming in to support you in your efforts. Zee Kay three-one-eight is already in touch with him."

One of the smaller suits of modern armor nodded, slightly. Lisa watched her, though she remained still until he dismissed them. She watched her lead the rest of them out, and didn't turn until the door had closed behind them.

"How many are there inside?" she asked.

"About a dozen at last count," Leo answered, moving to another exit.

"Let's put them down, and get out there to help."

There was a microsecond when he seemed ready to stop, and say something to her; then he began running along the wall, and she followed. Lisa could hear him answering the voice in his ear, whoever was feeding him information, but not the voice itself. They traversed corridors and stairwells until they came out on a lower floor. Howls filled the hallway as they opened the fire door, and they moved into position with practiced ease. They approached the sounds as quietly and quickly as possible, their armor giving them away as they moved. Peeking around a corner together, Lisa and Leo faced far more than a dozen howlers.

Several were feeding, or moving away from them and further up the hallway. Many had turned at the sounds of their clanking approach, and were waiting for them to round the corner.

Leo moved, stepping into the hallway and drawing his sword. Walking forward calmly, he met the first monster that moved with a rocket to its face. The creature stood in place for a moment, startled and headless, and dropped to the floor. Another rocket followed, and the assemblage exploded in all directions. Lisa fell into step beside her commander, and let loose a rocket from each wrist. Two howlers fell, bleeding out from the place where their heads used to be.

Another dashed forward, and Leo met it with cold steel. Stepping aside, he let the monster's own charge drag the blade nearly all the way through its neck. Leo held on, and finished the job before the creature could fall with a second rapid swing of the flashing blade. Lisa filled the hallway with automatic gunfire and explosive rockets while he moved forward once more, and drew her own sword from its scabbard. As one body they advanced through the smoke and rubble, beheading monsters and kicking at bodies. She heard a voice in the background, whooping and hollering something she couldn't quite make out. It was a moment before Lisa realized that she was hearing the voice in Leo's ear.

"Affirmative," Leo responded. "We've cleared the floor. We're heading to the next level."

They were halfway down the stairs when she heard the voice again; Lisa still couldn't make out the words, only a strangled cry. Leo didn't respond, and Lisa dismissed it until he hesitated at the fire door.

"Zee Kay three-one-eight," he said. It was customary for all of their communications between teams to sound in every helmet. Lisa felt her blood run cold at his next words.

"We've lost our eyes and ears," Leo said calmly. "Can you send two of your unit back to base? It sounds like we could use the backup."

"We can all come back, sir," Julia's voice was as measured as his.

Leo shook his head. "Two should be enough. Has the general arrived yet?"

"No, sir." Julia hesitated. "He encountered resistance en route. They are fighting their way to us."

"What is your situation?"

"Nothing we can't handle, sir," her voice came back quickly. "Blunt and Smiley will be with you soon."

"If it gets to be too much out there," Leo cautioned her, "then you need to fall back. We have plenty of room to house the general's people as well. This facility is made specifically for this situation."

There was a long pause before she replied. When she did, Julia's breath was coming in short quiet gasps.

"All due respect, sir," she shot back, "I was not trained in running or hiding. I was trained to put down this threat."

"Carry on," Leo replied calmly.

He pressed the release on the fire door, stepped boldly into the hallway. Arms outstretched, Leo released two rockets from his wrists before she got into position; back to back, they faced the threat as it converged on them from both sides up the hallway.

Explosions and automatic gunfire filled the air, along with bursts of flame and smoke. The suits kept their odor in, to protect them from detection; the ventilation system could handle nearly any kind of smoke or toxic gas, and deliver breathable air to the wearer. Somehow the smell didn't get filtered out with the smoke, and Lisa could taste the gunpowder and burning bodies.

"Fall back," Leo muttered. At first she thought he was still talking to Julia; his next words came, and she realized only her ears heard them.

"I'm out of rockets," he said.

Lisa pressed her right shoulder back against his left, turning their formation and pressing him toward the stairs. She lifted her arms as he had, pointing opposite directions down the hallway, and released two more explosive volleys. There was nothing but smoke and fire and tortured howls as she backed him into the stairs. They closed the fire door behind them, and started climbing.

"Blunt, Smiley, meet us at the ready room," Leo spoke as he cleared the steps four at a time. "We're low on ammo."

"I'll be there in ninety seconds, sir."

It was all he had to say, to be blunt; Smiley was gone. They came off the stairs, swords in hand, and burst into the hallway together. A high-pitched siren went off, and red lights flashed along the corridor.

"Security breach," an emotionless voice reported loudly. "Unauthorized entry."

"Blunt, tell me you keyed in the wrong code." Leo was frowning; she could hear it in his voice.

"Sir, no sir," Blunt's voice came back. "I'm well clear of the entrance. Want me to go back and secure it?"

"How's your ammo?"

"Out, sir." Blunt was frowning too. Lisa could hear it.

"Negative," Leo replied. "Proceed to the ready room. We'll secure the entrance together."

They were nearly reloaded when he burst through the door. When they were finished they helped him reload, and strapped as much explosive ammo to their suits as they could. Leo turned to her after, pointed at Lisa's locker.

"Can you show us the front door?" he asked.

Lisa nodded, opened the unlocked metal door and retrieved a device. It was about the size of a book, small enough to fit in someone's back pocket. She tapped the screen; it came alive with colors, and she tapped again. In moments she was holding the device up for him to see.

The front door was what they called it; it was actually a hallway, a long space between two sets of elevators. One elevator went up, to open in an ordinary-looking office building downtown. The other went down, into the facility. The stretch of hallway between them was empty.

"Can you back it up?"

Lisa positioned the device so they could see the image while she worked the control. They all watched a howler walking backward from the facility elevator to the front door. He walked in backward, and the door shut behind him.

"What the hell?" Lisa said. "What do they need to come in here for?"

"How do they even know we're here?" Leo added.

"You two have never been bitten," Blunt pointed out. "I have. The howler didn't just infect my body. It invaded my mind. There was a connection there, a link I couldn't sever. Like I was possessed."

Lisa turned to him. "Julia says it's even worse when you feed, and change again. She says it's like you become one with all of them;

you share their mind, and their hunger, as if it were your own."

"Chief talked to you about that?" Blunt asked her.

She nodded. "She said that what one howler knows, they all can know. They can see through each other's eyes, and into each other's thoughts. It's like one big hive mind."

"I've heard that," Leo said. "It's just so hard to imagine."

"Not if you've been bitten, sir." Blunt turned away.

"How's the situation out there?" Leo watched him until he turned, and answered the question.

"Pretty bad, sir," Blunt admitted. "The general isn't coming. Chief told him to withdraw and lock down his facility, that we had lost control of ours. They're trying to secure the block, but everyone's down to swords. Smiley did manage to clear an entire alley when he was taken out; the buildings collapsed around the explosion, giving them one less route in."

"And giving us one less way out," Leo said. "Alright, let's get to the front door and secure it."

They both heard him call out to her as they rode the express elevator from the ready room. Everyone whose suit was still on them could hear.

"Zee Kay three-one-eight, report your status."

There was a long silence, and the elevator door opened onto the hallway while they waited for a response. They filed into the hallway, taking up defensive positions immediately.

"We're in a holding pattern," her voice came back, finally. She was whispering. "They're being very cautious, sir; they won't engage unless we come out in the open, and we can't risk that."

"Can you fall back?" Leo asked. "If you can make it back here-"

"Negative, sir," she cut him off. "We're boxed in."

"We just restocked our ammunition," Leo told her, and they all heard. "There has been a breach at base. As soon as we contain and handle the threat we'll be coming for you."

"You should hurry up if you're coming," she came back. "We can't hold our position long. Best of luck, commander."

Lisa saw him stiffen in his suit. Her view of him was only peripheral; Leo was holding his position, and so was she. His head was tilted oddly, as if he were listening for something, or to something; Lisa heard nothing. Blunt was over her other shoulder, too far back to see. She kept her eyes on the elevator doors, her weapons at the ready. For several minutes they waited there; no more word came from the team. At last there was a sound, and a light.

The main elevator let out a muffled ding; Leo turned back towards it to watch the numbers on the glowing display climb to their floor. He didn't have to speak now; they all moved in closer to the metal doors. Lisa positioned herself directly in front of the elevator; Leo and Blunt were behind her, angled to fire past her if need be. She watched the numbers rise, visualizing herself putting down every one of these accursed monsters that had dared to rise. By the time the door opened Lisa knew that this was where the tide would turn. They would extinguish this threat, take back their team and then take back the base.

She could feel herself grinning malevolently when the metal whooshed aside. There was a moment of surprise when she saw Elayna in the box; the girl was covered in blood, but still unchanged. Between them was a monster, the biggest howler she had ever seen. Lisa's determination leapt to new heights within her, and she saw a chance to save the girl she'd been helping. Waiting for the monster to come at her, to present itself at an angle that didn't mean taking out Elayna, she activated the targeting laser on her wrist. Red dots appeared on the creature's thick armored forehead.

"You two aren't going anywhere," Lisa announced, stepping slightly aside and looking behind the howler. She winked at Elayna, though the girl couldn't see her through the mask. Lisa couldn't help but smile as she made her next statement, sharing her one-item list with the rest of the room.

"The zombie revolution is officially over," she said.

Lisa launched the missile.

ABOUT LEO'S HEART

The next story was started before the other two, as I stated earlier. It also led into the last story in another set, with a strong tie-in. That set was 'The Beginning of the End', which I wrote last. It was released second, though; it made way more sense to do it that way. If you've read that volume, you'll see the bridge between 'The Zombie Killers' and good old General Roberts right away as you get into this story. If you haven't read it… well, I heartily encourage you to do so. You don't have to stop right here and go back, or anything; I built the world of 'Zombie Zero' so it could be pieced together like a puzzle. Start with whatever pieces you want to start with; it will all come together in the end.

As soon as I met Leo, I liked him. As much as I might be a bit overly expressive in real life, I have always admired the strong and stoic figure. Leo showed me right away that the variance is not in how deeply you feel; it's just the expression that is different. That gave me an avenue to understanding him, and to him sharing his story with me.

My life has been unduly complicated a few times due to my habit of wearing my heart on my sleeve; but mostly it has been more enriching than encumbering. A guy like Leo could lose control of everything if he let himself be as guided by his emotions as I am, and seeing that helped me understand why he plays it so close to the vest.

As far as tie-ins...this has a bunch. It ties in with 'Tina's Bedside', the last short story from 'The Beginning of the End'. It ties in with Chapter Fourteen and Chapter Seventeen from 'The First Zombie'. Of course, it ties in with the two short stories that came before it in this book. In a way, it wraps up the set; in another way, that wrap-up actually really happens in Chapter Seventeen of 'The First Zombie'. If you've already filled in that piece of the puzzle, then you know how this ends. What you don't know yet is how it gets to that point, or why. That's what Leo is here to tell you, in his own reserved manner.

What never really gets addressed are the incredible risks that these people take just training for a day they hope never comes. Every time a new team member is recruited, they get a number. It's a deliberate reminder for Leo, of the ache that resides always in his big hidden heart. I hope you love his story!

LEO'S HEART

"Yes, General." Leo nodded. "I understand. How many do you need?"

They watched him, all eleven of the others, standing straight and still and silent. If any of them moved, the armor they wore would creak and clank; their weapons would slap against it, and would be even louder than the creaking and clanking. Yet none of them moved, and the room was filled with nothing but silence briefly broken by Leo's calm quiet voice. They stared straight ahead, lost in thought or paying perfect attention to the conversation, while he listened and replied to the earpiece.

"I'm sorry, General," Leo spoke again. "I don't have that many."

His voice was neither robotic nor emotional; there was no humor to his words, no sadness in his apology, no regret in the pronouncement. He listened to the response, and responded.

"Ten, sir," he said.

Leo stiffened, almost imperceptibly, listening. He shook his head.

"No, sir," Leo said. "I do not disagree."

His next words came quickly, a brief response to a short question.

"Yes, sir."

Leo looked at the gathering while he listened. His eyes found each of them, one at a time, then went on to the next. None of them moved, or met his gaze. When he was done, Leo fixed his eyes to a blank spot on the wall and spoke one last time.

"Of course, General," he said. "I feel the same, sir. Goodbye."

He pressed his earpiece, looked at each of them in turn once more.

"There is a facility near here," he said. "Zee Kay three-one-eight will stay here with me. The rest of you will go to this facility. It is a military installation that houses prisoners of war. There is a general there who has dealt with this kind of situation before. Treat him as you would treat me. He knows that his troops need further training; you will train them. Get what you need from your lockers, and get over there immediately. I will send the coordinates to Zee Kay three-two-seven. Be back here in seventy-two hours. Dismissed."

Their helmets clicked into place, they filed quickly out of the room. Leo watched them go.

"What about us?"

Leo paused. He didn't frown, but he wanted to. They had talked about being curt and professional at work, even if they were alone.

He looked at her, stone-faced, until she amended her sentence.

"What about us, sir?" she asked.

To her credit, the word was not even slightly touched by sarcasm. Leo loved that about her. Although she was not without humor, it was never a cutting humor. Leo didn't mind humor, like so many seemed to suppose; he just didn't like it when someone had to look the fool for someone else to get a laugh.

"We need to investigate the reported outbreak," Leo answered. "Let's get out of our suits and into street clothes. We're going to the airport."

*　*　*

Leo kept his eyes on the road and both hands on the wheel. The odometer needle stayed steady between traffic signals; his voice stayed calm as he answered her questions.

"Is it really happening?" she asked.

"It certainly looks like it," he responded.

He slowed to a stop before a red light, watched it until it turned green. The vehicle was powerful, but nearly silent; the only other sound in the car was the engine's low steady thrum.

"Every time we turn someone for a training exercise or to work on our cure," Leo said calmly. "The general knows immediately. Each time he turns one to work on his own reversal agent, we know immediately. Even one of these creatures creates a very distinctive electromagnetic signature; we saw five appear within an hour, in Africa, far from any lab or training facility. Four of them left immediately, on commercial airplanes; one disappeared from our sensors. The four flights are headed to major international airports around the world. One is coming here; we need to intercept her, and find out what is going on."

"Could it be a mistake?" she asked.

"That's what we're going to find out."

"Do you think it's a mistake?" she pressed.

"No." Leo navigated smoothly around a turn, accelerated to change lanes. "I think it's what we've all been training for, what we all hoped would never happen. It's the first natural transformation, and it happened outside any kind of containment. We've all seen how this spreads. Our only hope is to stop it before it starts here in our country."

"What about the rest of the world?" she breathed.

"They're on their own," Leo answered flatly. "If they know about this threat, they have not let on."

"Have we?" she asked. "Have we told any other countries what we know?"

Leo turned again, began following the signs to the airport terminal.

"Of course not," he said. "Can you imagine explaining that we need more money to fight zombies, to citizens or our allies? Or that everything we do is useless if there's an actual outbreak, but we can train them to do it too?"

They could see the terminal up ahead; Leo was looking for a place to put the car. She watched his serene face while he parked.

"You know that every new recruit thinks that you don't have a heart," she said. "It's not hard to see why, when you talk like that."

He curbed the wheels, slid the arm on the steering column until it stopped, and turned off the ignition. Leo left the keys in it. Still looking ahead, sitting motionless for a moment, he shrugged.

"I don't care what new recruits think of me," he said. "I don't care what anyone but the people I know and trust think of me."

She nodded. "And we all think you have an oversized heart. It's why you never smile, or frown; if you let the expressions start flowing, they'd never stop. You would spend all day hugging us and telling us all how proud you are of us, and we wouldn't get any training done. So you keep it locked inside, and let it drive you even harder."

He turned his head slowly, to meet her eyes. There was still no hint of an expression on his face. Leo knew it; he had practiced the look.

"Is that right?" he asked.

She smirked. "Am I wrong?"

Something in Leo shifted, or snapped. Tears filled his eyes, his expression softened, and he leaned toward her. He kissed her, softly.

"I love you, Lisa," Leo said.

There was no time to gauge her reaction; moments were slipping past. Leo collected himself, and exited the vehicle.

* * *

Leo was still staring at the lighted screen, watching the soft solitary glow. It had been his whole world for two days now, other than checking his mobile device for news updates every hour on the hour. Leo knew that was pointless; if it happened, he would know as quickly as everyone else. Still he checked, and tracked the slow movement in fifteen minute increments. Leo couldn't sleep; he watched the screen, hoping for fifteen minutes at a stretch. Each time the glow showed up, not far from where it had been last, and he let the tension go. Immediately it began to build again, his heart pounding harder and his breaths coming swift and shallow. Then the signature would show up, and he would sigh.

"Have you been here all this time?"

Leo turned at the sound, didn't register the words.

"Hey," he said, turning back to the screen. "I thought I told you to go home."

"I did what you ordered," Lisa responded, a little stiffly. "Did you hear me? Have you been here this whole time?"

He looked at his mobile device before answering, pressing the button that lit the screen and told him the time. Leo shook his head; even the date surprised him.

"Yeah." He nodded. "Yeah, I guess so. I can't believe it. She's still on the move, but she hasn't fed. She's slowing down, too. A lot. She's got to be twisted into a knot inside with hunger at this point."

Leo glanced at the screen, at his device.

"How are your folks?" he asked, looking up at her.

"They're fine," she said, glancing away. "All of the families are locked down in their outbreak shelters, waiting on word from one of us."

His eyes back on the screen, Leo nodded.

"How did everyone take it?" he asked.

"They were fine," she shrugged. "Some asked if they could be together, and I told them we had time. We moved supplies together, and got everyone secured."

"Did you tell them it was only precautionary?"

Leo turned when she didn't answer, held her gaze.

"What did you tell them?" he asked finally.

"I told them that this might be it, and it might not," Lisa shrugged again. "Those people are my family too. And they've seen the reports from Australia, and China, and South America. Maybe most people are in a state of shock and disbelief; they're not. Besides, I knew it would be best if some of them were...together. In case this is it."

"That's perfect." Leo put his eyes back on the screen, checked the location of the glow. "That's how the team would want it. It's why it works that so many of us are so close."

"It's not uncommon," Lisa pulled up a rolling seat, moved it so her arm touched his lightly. Leo didn't press into the contact; he didn't pull away either.

"A lot of special forces units bring their families together," Lisa continued, watching him watch the screen. "Fighter pilots are most notorious for it, since their mortality rates are so high. Many folks call it 'wife swapping', but that's ignorant."

"And sexist," Leo muttered, without turning. "Some of the best soldiers I've known have been women. I wouldn't doubt the same holds true for fighter pilots. Of course, I suppose they could have a wife as much as they could have a husband, now; but they couldn't have both. No one gets to have both. That is strictly forbidden by the laws of our government, no matter what the circumstances. As far as fighter pilot mortality rates are concerned, I envy them their survivability."

Lisa wouldn't let him steer away from it.

"Those people share more than their families, or their spouses," she said. "They share their lives; they share their love. They don't just want to know someone is there to take care of the people they love if they die; they want their every available minute to be full of that love. It's how they sustain through the most difficult of moments, and brave the most dangerous of missions; they know that even if they die, a part of them lives on in every member of that sacred family."

Leo turned, caught her gaze and held it.

"I need you to look at this," he told her.

Lisa frowned fiercely at him.

"I know you're worried," she said. "We should talk about this."

Leo shook his head. He pushed back his chair, pointed at the screen.

"Look," he insisted.

Lisa sighed, glanced over.

"That's fifteen minutes ago," he said. "Or somewhere within the last fifteen minutes. Now, look at this."

The screen flickered, stayed the same; the glow was in the same place. Other objects that showed up in the periphery of the monitor's tracking mode had moved; the brightest object had not.

"That's fifteen minutes earlier," he said. Leo heard the life coming back into his own voice. He clicked the pointer, and the screen flickered again. The glow had shifted, slightly.

"That's the previous fifteen minutes," he said.

Leo leaned back in his chair, watched her eyes go wide.

"She's not moving," she breathed.

"Not only that," Leo pointed, zoomed in on the map. "She's at a police station. Lisa, I think she might have turned herself in."

Her hand went to her pocket; with a swift series of swipes and taps, she got what she was looking for. She held the device up for him to see.

It was haunting, the black and white live feed. The ghastly figure was hunched over, her face hidden in shadow. Most of her hair had fallen out, along with several large pieces of flesh. Her skull showed through the veiny network of sinew that the camera was showing.

"She hasn't fed," Leo sighed.

Lisa tilted the device, looked at the digital stream.

"She looks awful," she said. "Like she hasn't eaten in weeks."

"Come on," Leo stood, pulled his jacket on and straightened his tie. "She must be fighting her hunger somehow. She won't last much longer."

*   *   *

Leo had lost all hope. He wasn't going to give up or anything; but reality was there, whether he faced it or not. There were too many; they had spread too far while the facility staff nursed the young woman back to human. They had developed a better cure, that worked faster, and an inoculation; the way things looked, it was too little too late. News reports were on every channel that was still broadcasting, and a single frame was all he needed to assess the situation. Leo's experienced eye had never lied to him before; now it told him there was no hope, and he believed it. He couldn't watch the team fall one by one; as the infection climbed into the facility somehow, Leo knew the countdown was over.

He called the general while he watched his team assemble in the ready room for the last time. Leo stood back as they filed in, keeping his body language as vague as possible. Working the communicator buttons imbedded in his glove, he scrolled through digital contact information on the inside of his helmet. None of them saw the digital scroll, or heard him when the call went through.

"General," he said. "I would like you to call Zee Kay three-one-eight, as soon as we get off the line. Get her coordinates and tell her you are on the way, if you would."

The general came right back, as calm and grave as Leo.

"Can do, Zee Kay zero-zero-one," he responded. "I'll get the troops ready to mobilize."

"Don't bother," Leo sighed. "Unless you have somewhere better to go. Tell her you are on the way; call back a little while later, and tell her you've been waylaid. The infected are everywhere; she knows it. It will come as no surprise. She'll probably tell you to fall back, and return to base. It will be easier if you never leave in the first place."

"It is that bad, then," the general said quietly. It wasn't a question; he had seen the same news reports, called the same phone numbers for answers. Everyone who had been anyone was long gone; their phones either no longer rang or went on forever without being picked up.

"You're our last hope, General," Leo said. "No pressure or anything."

"I don't know what I can do, commander," he answered.

"Lock down your facility, sir." His answer came back immediately. "Burn your dead upon pronouncement, and contain anyone who shows any signs of illness. After the worst passes, follow the coordinates that Zee Kay three-one-eight sends you. We've got a quicker cure, and an inoculation. Have your people find their way into the facility, and to the labs; everything you need to produce and distribute them is there."

"That's a tall order," the general pointed out. "And I'm an old man."

"Then I'll only ask one thing, sir." Leo paused, frowned against what he felt.

"Survive, sir," he said. "Just survive."

The general was the first to let his voice break, and rise in volume.

"Can you get here?" he asked suddenly. "There's no use in you dying. You or your people. Let's weather this together, Leo."

"That's very kind of you, Bill," Leo was still calm, though tears stood in his eyes. He blinked them away, glad for the mask and his strong steady voice. "We'd never make it. It was good to talk again, sir. Best of luck."

Leo cut the connection, thumbing the button on his glove. He could hear them now, and they him.

He looked them over, waiting until the team stood assembled and at attention. When Julia shifted slightly, he addressed them.

"We need to split up again," he told them. "Zee Kay three-two-seven and I will take back the facility; the rest of you need to take back the surrounding area. Stay close, and work together. You have all met General Roberts. His troops will be coming in to support you in your efforts. Zee Kay three-one-eight is already in touch with him."

He saw Julia nod. They filed out, and Leo watched them go. He resisted the urge to salute them, or call them back. Lisa was watching them as well; he scrolled to another contact and muted his speaker.

"Do you have eyes?" he asked.

"Yes, sir," the clipped voice came back. "There are approximately thirty howlers in the building; the largest concentration are on the floors two and three levels below you."

"Ten-four," Leo thumbed the switch. He turned to Lisa.

"How many are there inside?" she asked.

"About a dozen at last count," Leo lied. He moved toward the opposite doorway, and she followed.

"Let's put them down, and get out there to help," she said.

Leo paused, or he did in his mind; he imagined taking her hand, and telling her to wait. For the briefest of moments, he thought of telling her the truth, calling them all back and saving his family. But this was why he had a family in the first place; the people that he knew the best and loved the most were in his life because this day might eventually arrive. Now humanity was their family, and going down fighting was their duty. Let others run and hide; they were trained for this. It was their day, even if that meant it was their last day.

The moment was hardly a moment; in the next they were moving swiftly. Leo left his mask mute off while he communicated with the surveillance team, letting her hear his side of the exchange. He led her quickly down the passageway, following their brief clipped instructions.

"Go right," the voice told him. "Proceed until you can go right again."

"Right, right again," Leo repeated, for himself and for her. The voice came again as they took the second turn.

"Pass two left branch hallways, take the third." The voice paused, and Leo heard the sound of keyboard keys clicking quietly. "There are stairs to your right. I've disabled the security; it should open up without any need to swipe or key it."

"Third left," Leo echoed. "One and two and...I see the stairs. We're headed down."

"The second floor you'll come to is hot," the voice reminded him.

"Ten-four, eyes and ears," Leo nodded. "We're going down one more. We'll come back up after, then get up there to you."

"No hurry," came back briskly. "There's nothing anywhere near us. Once you contain those two floors, the facility is ours again."

"Good to hear," Leo put his hand on the doorknob. "Sit tight, we'll be back in control before you know it."

He could hear the other man breathing, faster than Leo. His words were less clipped and more uncertain as he spoke again.

"They're right around the corner, sir," he breathed. "Be careful, sir."

Leo nodded, assuming they were being watched as well. They were too close to them, and making too much noise already; and it was not a good idea to shut Lisa out right now. He took a quick peek around the corner, then stepped out into the hallway. He drew his sword. Lisa fell into position as he launched his first rocket. Another followed, between Lisa's launches; the hallway was filled with smoke, and screaming, as she brought her automatic pistols to bear. Leo listened to the man in his ear while he watched them fall and burn.

"Nice shot, sir!" The man sounded ecstatic. "Wow! You two are amazing! Look at that! Just a few more, sir! That's right! Oh, yeah! Oh, hell yeah! One more, sir, at one o'clock...yep, that's the one. That should be all of them, sir!"

"Affirmative," Leo responded. "We've cleared the floor. We're heading to the next level."

"Sir, yes sir!" The man was still giddy, and let out a few more triumphant exclamations. Then he stopped suddenly, and his voice grew very serious again.

"Uh, sir," he said quietly. "I've just picked up..."

His voice grew even more quiet, until he was scarcely whispering.

"Sir, we have activity on our-"

They were halfway to the next floor, but many flights from the surveillance room.

When Leo heard the man's strangled cry, followed by the wet sounds of frenzied feeding, he thumbed his communicator control.

"Zee Kay three-one-eight," he said. "We've lost our eyes and ears. Can you send two of your unit back to base? It sounds like we could use the backup."

"We can all come back, sir," Julia's responded.

Leo shook his head. "Two should be enough. Has the general arrived yet?"

"No, sir." Julia hesitated. "He encountered resistance en route. They are fighting their way to us."

"What is your situation?" Leo asked.

"Nothing we can't handle, sir," Julia responded. "Blunt and Smiley will be with you soon."

"If it gets to be too much out there," Leo told her, "then you need to fall back. We have plenty of room to house the general's people as well. This facility is made specifically for this situation."

She didn't say anything for several seconds. Leo's brow began to furrow as he waited; he opened his mouth to press her, just as she spoke.

"All due respect, sir," Julia gasped,

breathing heavy, "I was not trained in running or hiding. I was trained to put down this threat."

"Carry on," Leo smiled behind his mask. It was like she was in his mind. It had always been like that.

In the hallway, Leo let a rocket fly in either direction; there were howlers converging up the corridor on both sides, and they backed up to each other to clear each of them. Leo felt her shoulders pressing into his back with the recoil from her weapons; he let loose his last set of explosives, emptied his clip.

"Fall back," Leo muttered. "I'm out of rockets."

He thumbed the communicator pad when they were back in the quiet stairwell. Leo spoke while climbing.

"Blunt, Smiley, meet us at the ready room," he said. "We're low on ammo."

"I'll be there in ninety seconds, sir."

Leo thumbed himself into a muted silence; he swore at the omission, at the loss, at the first of his team to fall. He knew a number of words appropriate to the occasion, and he used them all. He was still cursing when the hall speaker sounded with a loud siren and a warning. Red lights began flashing at intervals along the corridor.

Leo fell silent.

"Security breach," a dispassionate voice said over the loudspeaker system. "Unauthorized entry."

Leo selected the channel that would let him talk to Blunt, thumbed off the mute so Lisa could hear.

"Blunt, tell me you keyed in the wrong code," Leo said.

He responded immediately. "Sir, no sir. I'm well clear of the entrance. Want me to go back and secure it?"

Leo hesitated. "How's your ammo?"

"Out, sir." To put it bluntly.

Leo felt himself frowning. He forced breath through his body, calm to his face. "Negative. Proceed to the ready room. We'll secure the entrance together."

When they were through the door, she went straight for his locker. Lisa loaded his suit with as much ammo as he could carry, talking as quickly as she moved. First she handed him rockets in pairs, then moved around his torso strapping more to his waist.

"We're going to put this threat down," she said. Leo checked the feed, to make sure it was only immediate audio; he didn't want the team to hear her. He wondered if she knew how panicked she sounded, and if pointing it out would help or hurt.

"We're going to take back the facility, and then the city." Lisa went on, rushing through words mindlessly as she clicked spare clips into place, took his empty weapons and handed them back full.

"Everything is going to be fine," she said, turning so he could arm her. "This is nothing more than a prologue to our happily ever after. All of us."

"I know," Leo nodded. He kept his voice as calm as possible. "You don't have to tell me. This is just another day at work, another bunch of hours to get through so we can be together."

"All of us," Lisa amended.

He nodded again.

"All of us," Leo echoed.

The door swung open, Blunt burst into the room.

"We're about done here," Leo said. "Lay out all the ammo you can carry on the bench; we'll get you loaded up."

Leo muted his mask, verified that their access to the team channel was blocked, and called out.

"Zee Kay three-one-eight," he said. "Report."

"Climber is down, sir," she said calmly,

immediately. "Swift is down as well. They both tried to clear us a path; it didn't work so well. Took out quite a few howlers, but they hemmed us in a little tighter too. Dancer's gearing up for an attempt. It sounds like a promising plan. Team out."

Leo knew that meant that she had to communicate with the unit, and couldn't tune them out right now; he understood. He cut the connection, and thumbed the mute off. Leo turned to Lisa.

He indicated her locker. "Can you show us the front door?"

Lisa opened the door and reached inside. The handheld device lit up at her touch, and with a few subtle motions she found what she was looking for. Lisa held it up for him to see.

There was nothing in the hallway; at least, not any more.

"Can you back it up?" he asked.

She moved so she could rewind the feed and let them see at the same time. In a few moments they all saw it, an oversized howler walking backward from one elevator to another.

"What the hell?" Lisa asked, still holding the image of the empty corridor. "What do they need to come in here for?"

Leo had a deeper concern. "How do they even know we're here?"

Blunt shook his head. "You two have never been bitten. I have. The howler didn't just infect my body. It invaded my mind. There was a connection there, a link I couldn't sever. Like I was possessed."

"Julia says it's even worse when you feed, and change again," Lisa added. "She says it's like you become one with all of them; you share their mind, and their hunger, as if it were your own."

"Chief talked to you about that?" Blunt sounded surprised.

Lisa nodded. "She said that what one howler knows, they all can know. They can see through each other's eyes, and into each other's thoughts. It's like one big hive mind."

Leo spoke. "I've heard that. It's just so hard to imagine."

Blunt turned from them. "Not if you've been bitten, sir."

"How's the situation out there?" Leo asked.

He watched Blunt, frowning, until he turned back.

"Pretty bad, sir," Blunt admitted. "The general isn't coming. Chief told him to withdraw and lock down his facility, that we had lost control of ours. They're trying to secure the block, but everyone's down to swords. Smiley did manage to clear an entire alley when he was taken out; the buildings collapsed around the explosion, giving them one less route in."

"And giving us one less way out," Leo pointed out. "Alright, let's get to the front door and secure it."

Leo opened the team channel, was glad that the others couldn't see the same digital display as he could. He gave Julia time to see that it was an open channel this time, and to consider her response. Leo made sure his voice was calm, his face serene. The three of them moved into the emergency express elevator as he spoke.

"Zee Kay three-one-eight, report your status."

She didn't come back until the elevator had let them out, and they had moved into position.

"We're in a holding pattern," Julia whispered. "They're being very cautious, sir; they won't engage unless we come out in the open, and we can't risk that."

"Can you fall back?" Leo asked. "If you can make it back here-"

Julia cut him off. "Negative, sir. We're boxed in."

"We just restocked our ammunition," Leo told them. "There has been a breach at base. As soon as we contain and handle the threat we'll be coming for you."

Julia paused, considering her answer. "You should hurry up if you're coming. We can't hold our position long. Best of luck, commander."

Leo felt himself frown, and he thumbed away all of the connections but hers. He muted his visor, and spoke to her.

"Julia?" he asked, tentatively.

"Yeah, Leo," she murmured. "It's just us."

"You're the only other one that knows," he said. "And you keep on fighting."

"We may have shared that secret before," Julia said. "I think the rest of the team knows at this point. It was clear that there were too few of us; the others probably saw it too. They just didn't say so."

"Like us," Leo said. "Maybe you're right; I don't think so, though. Lisa has been-"

Her laughter cut him off; it sounded sweet, and natural. Leo felt tears fill his eyes.

"Oh, not Lisa," Julia amended, still laughing. "She thinks that darkness is made from light somehow, and that determination makes magic. You know she thought we would see the day when the laws changed so we could love each other."

"The law never stopped my love." Leo felt a tear trickle down his cheek; it was a foreign feeling.

She laughed again, quieter this time. "I know. Me either."

Julia gasped, then swore fiercely.

"Did you see that?" she asked.

He had; two more of them had fallen, their names going dark on his visor readout. Julia didn't have a similar set-up; she and the other team members relied on him to link them in. He usually did, and the others likely thought that all team communication streams were shared. Leo was glad he had the option; no one heard them die, and only Julia saw it. And Julia...well, she could handle anything.

"Yeah," Leo answered. "I saw."

"I should go," Julia said softly. "Were you trying to say goodbye?"

"I never said hello to you," Leo mused, just as quietly. "I held off getting attached to you; I thought you'd break. I thought you were an egg ready to crack, hard on the outside and all gooey on the inside."

Her laugh was tense, swift.

"Not me, Leo," she said. "You're the one that's all gooey on the inside. You don't fool me, lover. You never did. About anything."

"I know." Leo's voice was almost not even there. "Hello, Julia."

"Hello, Leo." Julia's voice was getting stronger, louder. "It is an honor to be dedicated to your commitment. No regrets, Leo; and no goodbyes. We live true to ourselves, until we live no longer."

He saw her visor sound go live, and he patched her in to the rest of her field team. Leo listened, without letting them know he could hear, as they fell one by one. He heard Julia shout orders, and hope, between screams and howls and the sounds of slashing blades. Leo let the tears fall with his family, and watched the lighted names turn dark on his digital display. She was the last one standing; he listened to Julia shout challenges at monsters, heard her hack at them with her sword; then she was silent, and the only sound in his helmet was his own heartbeat pounding in his ears.

Leo shifted when he saw the lighted panel above the elevator door glow brighter. He watched the numbers rise while he listened to Julia's movements. She released her helmet, and tossed it nearby; Leo could hear her fighting, and then feeding. When he heard her howl, he almost shut off the feed;

as the elevator neared, he waited. Footsteps sounded, getting closer to the helmet. She spoke into it, though it didn't sound as though she put it back on.

"Self-destruct code nine."

Her voice was twisted, grating, monstrous.

"Activate."

Leo heard the voice begin almost as soon as hers ended.

"Ten." The voice had no humanity, no compassion, no understanding of what it was foretelling.

"Nine." A hungry howl sounded, and another answered; it was cut off, and replaced by the frenzied sounds of one monster tearing another apart.

"Eight."

Leo shut off the feed, thumbed the mute button and filled his helmet with the tense sounds of waiting. The tears on his face had dried.

Dear reader,

Alright, I get it...things got a little grim from time to time in these stories. It was a bit tough to avoid, while writing about a zombie apocalypse. I hope you enjoyed the stories, and the commentary between, and that you'll be coming back to collect all the other pieces that make up the 'Zombie Zero' puzzle. With two main books and six short story volumes, I applied my big picture attitude to building this world. Nothing thrills me more than the thought of you loving every volume in its own way, and for your own reasons, just like I do.

'The Secret Society of Deeper Meaning' is a great way to make sure you don't miss anything from me. If you join up, you'll get all kinds of member only content while also being automatically entered in all the monthly giveaways. You'll also be a member of my favorite secret society ever, and get a weekly message from me; and it's all free!

If you've already joined up, thank you! You should know how much you mean to me. (Or you should start reading your emails.) If belonging to a secret society is too much for you, but you really want to proclaim your love for this book, you could also review it.

I appreciate reviews so much, I posted a tutorial on writing them on my website to help folks that might need a little guidance. Check it out, if you want, to see how little it takes to really help an author you enjoy and other readers like you at the same time.

Some folks might not feel comfortable posting publicly. Writing me a quick email to tell me that you loved one of my books is always an option, and I appreciate every message I receive more than I can express without getting all blubbery. (If you want that, you'll have to sign up for the newsletter.) I'm busy...but be patient, I'll get back to you.

The most important thing you can do to help me is the thing you just did, which is read one of my books. I say that I hope you love these stories because I quite frankly hope you love these stories. My biggest hope is that you loved them enough to want more from me, and that this is not the last time our minds will meet like this.

For now, I'll thank you one last time, for that most important of things...

Thanks for reading!

All the best,

Jay

Jay@JayNorry.com

Twitter: @JayNorry

Also available from J.K. Norry. . .

<u>Zombie Zero</u>
Zombie Zero: The First Zombie
Zombie Zero: The Last Zombie

<u>Zombie Zero: The Short Stories</u>
Volume 1: The Sickness Spreads
Volume 2: The Beginning of the End
Volume 3: Love Lost at Sea
Volume 4: The Zombie Killers
Volume 5: Monstrous Consequences
Volume 6: The Heart of the Monster

<u>The Walking Between Worlds trilogy</u>
Demons & Angels (Book I)
Rise of the Walker King (Book II)
Fall of the Walker King (Book III)

<u>As Jay Norry</u>
Stumbling Backasswards Into the Light

Learn more about the author at
www.JayNorry.com

www.ingramcontent.com/pod-product-compliance
Lightning Source LLC
Chambersburg PA
CBHW051710180726
48283CB00004B/1285